Rock Manning Goes For Broke

CHARLIE JANE ANDERS

Subterranean Press 2018

First Edition

ISBN
978-1-59606-878-0

Subterranean Press
PO Box 190106
Burton, MI 48519

subterraneanpress.com

Manufactured in the United States of America

for d.g.k. goldberg

1.

BREAK! BREAK! BREAK!

Earliest I remember, Daddy threw me off the roof of our split-level house. "Boy's gotta learn to fall sometime," he told my mom just before he slung my pants seat and let go. As I dropped, Dad called out instructions, but they tangled in my ears. I was four or five. My brother caught me one-handed, gave me a spank, and dropped me on the lawn. Then up to the roof for another go round, with my body more slack this time.

From my dad, I learned there were just two kinds of bodies: falling, and falling on fire.

My dad was a stuntman with a left-field resemblance to an actor named Jared Gilmore who'd been in some TV show before I was born, and he'd gotten it in his head Jared was going to be the next big action movie star. My father wanted to be Jared's personal stunt double and "prosthetic acting device," but Jared never responded to the letters, emails and Web sites, and Dad got a smidge persistent, which led to some restraining orders and blacklisting. Now he was stuck in the boonies doing stunts for TV movies about people who survive accidents. My mama did data entry to cover the rest of the rent. My dad was determined that my brother Holman and I would know the difference between a real and a fake punch, and how to roll with either kind.

My life was pretty boring until I went to school. School was so great! Slippery just-waxed hallways, dodgeball, sandboxplosions, bullies with big elbows, food fights! Food fights! If I could have gone to school for twenty hours a day, I would have signed up. No, twenty-three! I only ever really needed one hour of sleep per day. I didn't know who I was and why I was here until I went to school. And did I mention authority figures? School had authority figures! It was so great!

I love authority figures. I never get tired of pulling when they push, or pushing when they pull. In school, grown-ups were always telling me to write on the board, and then I'd fall down or drop the eraser down my pants by mistake, or misunderstand and knock over a pile of giant molecules. Erasers are comedy gold! I was kind of a hyper kid. They tried giving me ritalin ritalin ritalin ritalin riiiitaliiiiin, but I was one of the kids who only gets more hyper hyper on that stuff. Falling, in the seconds between up and down, you know what's going on. People say something is as easy as falling off a log, but really it's easy to fall off anything. Really, try it. Falling rules!

Bullies learned there was no point in trying to fuck me up, because I would fuck myself up faster than they could keep up with. They tried to trip me up in the hallways, and it was just an excuse for a massive set piece involving mops, stray book bags, audio/video carts and skateboards. Limbs flailing, up and down trading places, ten fingers of mayhem. Crude stuff. I barely had a sense of composition. Every night until three a.m., I sucked up another stack of Buster Keaton, Harold Lloyd or Jackie Chan movies on the ancient laptop my parents didn't know I had, under my quilt. Safety Last!

Ricky Artesian took me as a personal challenge. A huge guy with a beachball jaw—he put a kid in the hospital for a month in fifth grade for saying anybody who didn't ace this one chemistry quiz had to be a dipshit. Some time after that, Ricky stepped to me with a Sharpie in the locker room and slashed at my arms and ribcage, marking the bones he wanted to break. Then he walked away, leaving the whole school whispering, "Ricky Sharpied Rock Manning!" I hid when I didn't have class, and when school ended, I ran home three miles to avoid the bus. I figured Ricky would try to get me in an enclosed space where I couldn't duck and weave, so I stayed wide open. If I needed the toilet, I swung into the stall through a ventilator shaft and got out the same way, so nobody saw me enter or leave. The whole time in the airshaft, my heart cascaded. This went on for months, and my whole life became not letting Ricky Artesian mangle me. One day I got careless and went out to the playground with the other kids during recess, because some teacher was looking. I tried to watch for trouble, but a giant hand swooped down from the swingset and hauled me up. I dangled a moment, then the hand let me fall onto the sand. I fell on my back and started to get up, then Ricky told me not to move. For some reason, I did what he said, even though I saw twenty-seven easy ways out of that jungle-gym cage, and then Ricky stood over me. He told me again to hold still, then brought down one boot on the long bone of my upper arm, a clean snap, my reward for staying put. "Finally got that kid to quit hopping," I heard him say as he walked across the playground. Once my arm healed up, I became a crazy frog again, and Ricky didn't bother me.

Apart from that one stretch, my social life at school was ideal. People cheered for me but never tried to talk to me—it was the best of human interaction without any of the pitfalls. Ostracism, adulation: flipsides! They freed me to orchestrate gang wars and alien invasions in my head, whenever I didn't have so many eyes on me. Years passed, my mom tried to get me into dance classes, my dad struggled to get me to take falling down seriously as a noble struggle with gravity, the way my big brother did. Holman was spending every waking moment prepping for the Army, which was his own more socially acceptable way of rebelling against Dad.

Sally Hamster threw a brick at my head. I'd barely noticed the new girl in my class, except she was tall for a seventh grader and had big Popeye arms. I felt the brick coming before I heard it, then people shouting. Maybe Sally just wanted to get suspended, maybe she was reaching out. The brick grazed my head, but I was already moving with it, forward into a knot of basketball players, spinning and sliding. Afterwards I had a lump on my head but I swore I'd thrown the brick at myself. By then the principal would have believed almost anything of me.

I didn't get the *Krazy Kat* reference until years later, but Sally and I became best friends. We sketched lunch-trolley incidents and car pile-ups in our heads, talking them out during recess, trading text messages in class, instant messaging at home. The two of us snuck out to the Winn Dixie parking lot and Sally drilled me for hours on that Jackie Chan move where the shopping trolley rolls at him and he swings inside it through the flap, then jumps out the top. I didn't know martial arts, but I practiced not being run over by a shopping cart over and over. We went to the big mall off I-40 and got ourselves banned from the sporting goods store and the Walmart, trying to stage the best accidents. Sally shouted instructions: "Duck! Jump! Now do that thing where your top half goes left and your bottom half goes right!" She'd throw dry goods, or roll barrels at me, and then shout, "Wait, wait, wait, go!" Sally got it in her head I should be able to do the splits, so she bent my legs as far apart as they would go and then sat on my crotch until I screamed, every day for a couple months.

The Hamster family had social aspirations, all about Sally going to Harvard and not hanging out with boys with contrarian extremities. I went over to their house a few times, and it was full of Buddhas and Virgin Marys, and Mrs. Hamster baked us rugelachs and made punch, all the while telling me it must be So Interesting to be the class clown but how Sally needed to laser-beam in on her studies. My own parents weren't too thrilled about all my school trouble, and why couldn't I be more like Holman, training like crazy for his military future?

High school freshman year, and Sally got hold of a video cam. One of her jag-tooth techno-hippie uncles. I got used to her being one-eyed, filming all the time, and editing on the fly with her mom's hyperbook. Our first movie went online at Yourstuff a month after she got the camera. It was five minutes long and it was called *The Thighcycle Beef*, which was a joke on some Italian movie Sally had seen. She had a Thighcycle, one of those bikes which goes nowhere with a lying odometer. She figured we could light it on fire and then shove it off a cliff with me riding it, which sounded good to me.

I never flashed on the whole plot of *The Thighcycle Beef*, but there were ninja dogs and exploding donuts and things. Like most of our early short films it was a mixture of live-action and Zap!mation. Sally figured her mom would never miss the Thighcycle, which had sat in the darkest basement corner for a year or so. We did one big sequence of me pedaling on the Thighcycle with Sally throwing rocks at me, which she would turn into throwing stars in post-production. I had to pedal and duck, pedal while hanging off the back wheel, pedal side-saddle, pedal with my hands while hanging off the handlebars, etc. I climbed a tree in the Hamsters' front yard and Sally hoisted the Thighcycle so I could pull it up there with me. Then I climbed on and "rode" the Thighcycle down from the treetop, pedaling frantically the whole way down as if I could make it fly. (She was going to make it fly in post.) The Thighcycle didn't pedal so good after that, but Sally convinced me I was only sprained because I could scrunch all my fingers and toes and I didn't lose consciousness for that long. We were going to film the climax at a sea-cliff a few miles away, but Sally's ride fell through. In the end, she settled for launching me off the tool shed with the Thighcycle on fire. She provided a big pile of leaves for me to fall onto when I fell off the cycle, since I already had all those sprains. I missed the leaf pile, but the flaming Thighcycle didn't, and things went somewhat amiss, although we were able to salvage some of the toolshed thanks to Sally having the garden hose ready. She was amazingly safety-minded.

After that, Sally's parents wanted twice as hard for her not to see me. I had to lie and tell my parents I'd sprained my whole body beating up a bunch of people who deserved it. My brother had to carry stuff for me while I was on crutches, which took away from his training time. He kept running ahead of me with my junk, lecturing me about his conspiracy theories about the Pan-Asiatic Ecumen, and how they were flooding the United States with drugs to destabilize our country and steal our water, and I couldn't get out of earshot.

But all of my sprains were worth it, because *Thighcycle Beef* blew up the Internet. The finished product was half animation, with weird messages like "NUNCHUCK SPITTING TIME!" flashing on the screen in between, but the wacky stunts definitely helped. She even turned the toolshed into a cliff, although she also used the footage of the toolshed fire elsewhere. People two or three times our age downloaded it to their ipods and phones and watched it at work. Sally showed me the emails, tweets and Yangars—we were famous!

I found out you can have compound sprains just like fractures, and you have to eat a lot of ice cream and watch television while you recuperate. My mom let me monopolize the living-room sofa, knitted blanket over my legs and formica tray in my lap as I watched cartoons. My mom wanted to watch the news, the water crisis and the debt crisis were freaking her shit. I wanted to catch the Sammo Hung marathon, but she kept changing to CNN, people tearing shopping malls apart with their bare hands in Florida, office windows shattering in Baltimore, buses on fire. And shots of emaciated people in the formerly nice part of Brooklyn, laying in heaps with tubes in their arms, to leave a vein permanently open for the next hit. Did I mention ice cream? I got three flavors, or five if you count Neopolitan as three separate flavors, like all right-thinking people everywhere.

I went back to school after a week off, and the Thighcycle had a posse. Ricky—femur-cracking Ricky Artesian—came up to me and said our movie rocked his freaking head. He also said something about people like me having our value, which I didn't pay much attention to at the time. I saw one older kid in the hallway with a Flaming Thighcycle T-shirt, which I never saw any royalties.

Sally snuck out to meet me at the Starbucks near school and we toasted with frosty mochas. Her round face looked sunburned and her hair was a shade less mouse than usual. "That was just the dry run," she said. "Next time, we're going to make a statement. Maybe we can go out to the landfill and get a hundred busted TVs and drop them on you." I vetoed the rain of TVs. I wanted to do a roller disco movie because I'd just watched *Xanadu*. We posted on Yangar.com looking for roller-disco extras, and a hundred kids and a few creepy grown-ups hit us back. We had to be super selective, and mostly only took people who had their own skates. But Sally still wanted to have old televisions in there because of her Artistic Vision, so she got hold of a dozen fucked old screens and laid them out for us to skate over while they all showed the same footage of Richard Simmons. We had to jump over beach balls and duck under old power cords and stuff. I envisioned it being the saga of skate-fighters who were trying to bring the last remaining copy of the U.S. Constitution to the federal government in hiding, in a bunker under a Chikken Hut. We filmed a lot of it at an actual Chikken Hut that had closed down off near the Oceanview Mall. I wanted it to be a love story, but we didn't have a female lead, and also Sally never wanted to do love stories. I showed her Harold Lloyd movies but it made no difference.

Sally got hooked on Yangar fame. She had a thousand Yangar friends, crazy testimonials and imitators from Pakistan, and it all went to her head. We had to do what the people on the Internet wanted us to do, even when they couldn't agree. They wanted more explosions, more costumes and cute Zap!mation icons, funny catch phrases. At fifteen, Sally breathed market research. I wanted pathos *and* chaos!

Ricky and some other kids found the school metal detectors missed anything plastic, ceramic, wood or bone, and soon they had weapons strapped all over. Ricky was one of the first to wear the red bandana around his neck, and everyone knew he was on his way. He shattered Mr. MacLennan's jaw, my Geography teacher, right in front of our whole grade in the hallway. Slow-time, a careful spectacle, to the point where Ricky let the onlookers arrange ourselves from shortest in front to tallest in back. Mr. MacLennan lying there looking up at Ricky, trying to assert, while we all shouted Break! Break! Break! Break! and finally Ricky lifted a baseball bat and I heard a loud crack. Mr. MacLennan couldn't say anything about it afterwards, even if he could have talked, because of that red bandana.

Sally listened to the police scanner, sometimes even in the classroom, because she wanted to be there right after a looting or a credit riot. Not that these things happened too often in Alvington, our little coastal resort city. But one time, Sally got wind a Target near downtown had gone crazy. The manager had announced layoffs and the staff just started trashing the place, and the customers joined in. Sally came to my math class and told Mr. Pope I'd been called to the principal's, and then told me to grab my bag of filming crap and get on my bike. What if we got there and the looters were still going? But Sally said looting was not a time-consuming process, and the crucial thing was to get there between the looting and everything being chained up. So we got there and sneaked past the few cops buddying in the parking lot, so Sally could get a few minutes of me falling under trashed sporting goods and jumping over clothing racks. She'd gotten so good at filming with one hand and throwing with the other! Really nobody ever realized she was the coordinated one, of the two of us. Then the cops chased us away.

My brother got his draft notice and couldn't imagine such luck. He'd sweated getting into the Army for years, and now they weren't even waiting for him to sign up. I knew my own draft notice was probably just a year or two down the line, maybe even sooner. They kept lowering the age.

My mom's talk shows were full of people saying we had to stop the flow of drugs into our country, even if we had to defoliate half the planet. If we could just stop the drugs, then we could fix our other problems, easy. The problem was, the Pan-Asiatic Ecumen or whoever was planting these drugs were too clever for us, and they had gotten hold of genetically engineered opioids that they could grow in vats, like brewer's yeast, and they had 900 times the potency of regular junk. We tried using drones to take down all their drug labs, but they just relocated to heavily populated areas, and soon it was block-by-block urban warfare in a dozen slums all around Eurasia. Soldiers were fitted with cheap mass-produced HUDs that made the whole thing look like a first-person shooter from 40 years ago. Some people said the Pan-Asiatic Ecumen didn't actually exist, but then how else did you explain the state we were in?

Sally fell in love with a robot guy named Raine, and suddenly he had to be big in every movie. She found him painted silver on Main street, his arms and legs moved all blocky and she thought he had the extra touch we needed. In our movies, he played Castle the Pacifist Fighting Droid, but in real life he clutched Sally's heart in his cold unbreakable metal fist. He tried to nice up to me, but I saw through him. He was just using Sally for the Yangar fame. I'd never been in love, because I was waiting for the silent-movie love: big eyes and violins, chattering without sound, pure. Nobody had loved right since 1926.

Ricky Artesian came up to me in the cafeteria early on in eleventh grade. He'd gotten so he could loom over *and* around everybody. I was eating with Sally, Raine and a few other film geeks, and Ricky told me to come with him. My first thought was, whatever truce we'd made over my arm-bone was over and gone, and I was going to be fragments of me. But Ricky just wanted to talk in the boys room. Everyone else cleared out, so it was just the two of us and the wet TP clinging to the tiles. The air was sour. "Your movies, they're cool," he said. I started to explain they were also Sally's, but he hand-slashed.

"My people." He gestured at the red bandana. "We're going to take it all down. They've lied to us, you know. It's all fucked, and we're taking it down." I nodded, not so much in agreement, but because I'd heard it before. "We want you to make some movies for us. Explaining what we're about."

I told him I'd have to ask Sally, and he whatevered, and didn't want to listen to how she was the brains, even though anyone looking at both of us could tell she was the brains. Ricky said if I helped him, he'd help me. We were both almost draft-age, and I would be a morning snack to the military exoskeletons. I'd seen *No Time For Sergeants*—seventeen times—so I figured I knew all about basic training, but Ricky said I'd be toast. Holman had been telling me the same thing, when he wasn't trying to beat me up. So Ricky offered to get me disqualified from the Army, or get me under some Protection during training.

When I told Sally about Ricky's offer, the first thing she did was ask Raine what he thought. Raine wasn't a robot that day, which caught me off-guard.

He was just a sandy-haired flag-eared skinny guy, a year or so older than us. We sat in a seaside gazebo/pagoda where Sally thought she could film some explosions. Raine said propaganda bad, but also could Ricky get him out of the army as well as me? I wasn't sure. Sally didn't want me to die, but artistic integrity, you know.

The propaganda versus artistic integrity thing, I wasn't sure about. How was making a movie for Ricky worse than pandering to our fans on Yourstuff and Yangar? And look, my dad fed and housed Holman and me by arranging tragic accidents for cable TV movies where people nursed each other back to health and fell in love. Was my dad a propagandist because he fed people sponge cake when the whole world was flying apart?

Sally said fine, shut up, we'll do it if you just stop lecturing us. I asked Ricky and he said yes, neither Raine nor I would have to die if we made him a movie.

This was the first time we ever shot more footage than we used. I hadn't understood how that could happen. You set things up, boom! you knocked them over and hoped the camera was running, and then you moved on somewhere else. Life was short, so if you got something on film, you used it! But for the red bandana movie we shot literally hundreds of hours of footage to make one short film. Okay, not literally hundreds of hours. But a few.

Raine didn't want to be the Man, or the Old Order, or the Failure of Democracy, and I said tough shit. Somebody had to, plus he was older and a robot. He and Sally shot a ton of stuff where they humanized his character and explained how he thought he was doing the right thing, but we didn't use any of it in the final version. Meanwhile, I wore the red bandana and breakdanced under a rain of buzzsaws that were really some field hockey sticks we'd borrowed. I, too, wanted to humanize my character by showing how he only donned the red bandana to impress a beautiful florist, played by Mary from my English class. After a few weeks' filming, we started to wonder if maybe we should have had a script. "We never needed one before," Sally grumbled. She was pissed about doing this movie, and I was pissed that she kept humanizing her boyfriend behind my back. You don't humanize a robot! That's why he's a robot instead of a human!

Holman came back from basic training, eager to show us the scar behind his left ear where they'd given him a socket that his HUD would plug into. It looked like the knot of a rotten tree, crusted with dried gunk and with a pulsating wetness at its core. It wasn't as though they would be able to remote-control you or anything, Holman said—more like, sometimes in a complicated mixed-target urban environment, you might hesitate to engage for a few crucial split seconds and the people monitoring the situation remotely might need to guide your decision-making. So to speak. Holman seemed happy for the first time ever, almost stoned, as he talked us through all the crazy changes he'd gone through in A.N.V.I.L. training and how he'd learned to breathe mud and spit bullets. Holman was bursting with rumors about all the next-generation weapons that were coming down the pike, like sonic cannons that could shatter everything for miles.

Ricky kept asking to see the rushes of our movie, and Raine got his draft notice, and we didn't know how the movie was supposed to end. I'd never seen any real propaganda before. I wanted it to end with Raine crushing me under his shiny boot, but Sally said it should end with me shooting out of a cannon (which we'd make in Zap!mation) into the Man's stronghold (which was the crumbling Chikken Hut) and then everything would blow up. Raine wanted the movie to end with his character and mine joining forces against the real enemy, the Pan-Asiatic Ecumen, but Sally and I both vetoed that. In the end, we filmed like ten different endings and then mashed them all up. Then we added several Zap!mation only characters, and lots of messages on the screen like, "TONGUE-SAURUS!" and "OUTRAGEOUS BUSTAGE!" My favorite set piece involved me trying to make an ice cream sundae on top of a funeral hearse going 100 mph, while Sally threw rocks at me. (I forget what we turned the rocks into, after.) There was some plot reason I had to make a sundae on top of a hearse, but we borrowed an actual hearse from this guy Raine knew who worked at a funeral home, and it actually drove 100 mph on the cliffside road, with Sally and Raine driving alongside in Raine's old Prius. I was scooping ice cream with one hand and squirting fudge with the other, and then Sally beaned me in the leg and I nearly fell off the sea-cliff, but at the last minute I caught one of the hearse's rails and pulled myself back up, still clutching the full ice-cream scoop in the other hand. With ice cream, all things are possible.

The final movie clocked in at twelve minutes, way way longer than any of our previous efforts. It was like an attention-span final exam. We showed it to Ricky in Tanner High's computer room, on a bombed-out old Mac. I kept stabbing his arm, pointing out good parts like the whole projectile rabies bit and the razor-flower-arranging duel that Raine and I get into towards the end. Ricky seemed to hope that if he spun in his chair and then looked back at the screen, this would be a different movie. Sometimes he would close his eyes, bounce, and reopen them, then frown because it was still the same hot sewage.

By the time the credits rolled, Ricky seemed to have decided something. He stood up and smiled, and thanked us for our great support for the movement, and started for the door before we could even show him the "blooper reel" at the end. I asked him about our draft survival deal, and he acted as if he had no clue what we were talking about. Sally, Raine and I had voluntarily made this movie because of our fervent support of the red bandana and all it stood for. We could post the movie online, or not, it was up to us, but it had nothing to do with Ricky either way. It was weird seeing Ricky act so weaselly and calculating, like he'd become a politician all of a sudden. The only time I saw a hint of the old Ricky was when he said he'd use our spines as weed-whackers if we gave any hint that he'd told us to make that movie.

The blooper reel fizzed on the screen, unnoticed, while Raine, Sally and I stared at each other. "So this means I have to die after all?" Raine said in his robotic stating-the-obvious voice. Sally didn't want to post our movie on the Internet, even after all the work we'd put into it, because of the red-bandana thing. People would think we'd joined the movement. Raine thought we should post it online, and maybe Ricky would still help us. I didn't want to waste all that work—couldn't we use Zap!mation to turn the bandana into, say, a big snake? Or a dog collar? But Sally said you can't separate a work of art from the intentions behind it. I'd never had any artistic intentions in my life, and didn't want to start having them now, especially not retroactively. First we didn't use all our footage, and then there was talk of scripts, and now we had intentions. Even if Raine hadn't been scheduled to go die soon, it was pretty obvious we were done.

I tried telling Raine that he might be okay, the Pan-Asiatic Ecumen could surrender any time now and they might call off the draft. Or, and here was an idea that I thought had a lot of promise, Raine could work the whole "robot" thing and pretend the draft didn't apply to him because he wasn't a person, but Sally told me to shut the fuck up. Sally kept jumping up and down, cursing the air and hitting things, and she threatened to kick the shit out of Ricky. Raine just sat there slump-headed, saying it wasn't the end of the world, maybe. We could take Raine's ancient Prius, load it up, and run for Canada, except what would we do there?

We were getting the occasional email from Holman, but then we realized it had been a month since the last one. And then two months. We started wondering if he'd been declared A.U.T.U.— and in that case, if we would ever officially find out what had happened to him.

A few days before Raine was supposed to report for death school, there was going to be a huge anti-war protest in Raleigh, and so we drove all the way there with crunchy bars and big bottles of grape sprocket juice, so we'd be sugared up for peace. We heard all the voices and drums before we saw the crowd, then there was a spicy smell and we saw people of twenty different genders and religions waving signs and pumping the air and chanting old-school style about what we wanted and when we wanted it. A platoon of bored cops in riot gear stood off to the side. We found parking a couple blocks away from the crowd, then tried to find a cranny to slip into with our signs. We were looking around at all the other objectors, not smiling but cheering, and then I spotted Ricky a dozen yards away, in the middle of a lesbian posse. And a few feet away from him, another big neckless angry guy. I started seeing them everywhere, dotted throughout the crowd. They weren't wearing the bandanas, they were blending in until they got some kind of signal. I grabbed Sally's arm. "Hey, we have to get out of here."

"What the fuck are you talking about? We just got here!"

I pulled at her. It was hard to hear each other with all the bullhorns and loudspeakers, and the chanting. "Come on! Grab Raine, this is about to go crazy. I'll make a distraction."

"It's always about you making a distraction! Can't you just stop for a minute? Why don't you just grow the fuck up? I'm so sick of your bull-shit. They're going to kill Raine, and you don't even care!" I'd never seen Sally's eyes so small, her face so red.

"Sally, look over there, it's Ricky. What's he doing here?"

"What are you talking about?"

I tried to pull both of them at once, but the ground had gotten soddy from so many protes-tor boots and I slipped and fell into the dirt. Sally screamed at me to stop clowning around for once, and then one of the ISO punks stepped on my leg by mistake, then landed on top of me and the crowd was jostling the punk as well as me, so we couldn't untangle ourselves. Someone else stepped on my hand. I rolled away from the punk and sprang upright just as the first gunshot sounded. I couldn't tell who was firing, or at what, but it sounded nearby. Everyone in the crowd shouted without slogans this time and I went down again with boots in my face. I saw a leg that looked like Sally's and I tried to grab for her. More shots, and police bullhorns calling for us to surrender. Forget getting out of here, we had to stay down even if they trampled us. I kept seeing Sally's feet but I couldn't reach her. Then a silver shoe almost stepped on my face. I stared at the bright laces a second, then grabbed at Raine's silvery ankle, but he wouldn't go down because the crowd held him up. I got upright and came face-to-shiny-face with Raine. "Listen to me," I screamed over another rash of gunfire. "We have to get Sally, and then we have to—"

Raine's head exploded. Silver turned red and my mouth was suddenly full of something warm and dark-tasting, and then several people fleeing in opposite directions crashed into me and I swallowed. I swallowed and doubled over as the crowd smashed into me, and I forced myself not to vomit because I needed to be able to breathe. Then the crowd pushed me down again and my last thought was that with this many extras, all we really needed would be a crane and a few dozen skateboards and we could have had a really cool set piece.

2.

VIKINGS VS. STEAMPUNKS

Sally's face had gotten rounder and brighter since high school, and her hair was a bright crimson swoosh across her forehead. She wore a big black trenchcoat, shorts and hiking boots. Next to her stood a skinny African American woman named Janelle, in a FREE YUSUF T-shirt and hoop skirt. They went to film school together, and they had their own private language about *mise en scene*. They were collaborating on a movie about a woman (played by Janelle) who thinks her cat is talking to her. Sally and Janelle lived with a few other people in a rambledown house just off the main drag in Jamaica Plain. Outside, the house looked slanty and weatherbeaten, but inside it had clean carpets, oak furniture and huge film posters in metal frames. Sally walked ahead of us as we moved into her house, so she could move vases and bowls of fruit out of my reach, then she got to work making dinner. I offered to help with the cooking, but she didn't need any. All of a sudden in her vinyl apron she reminded me of Mrs. Hamster: smiling with one shoulder hunched and tense lines etched in her arms and waist, stirring and cutting.

I'd come up to Boston with this idea that lightning would strike, Sally would take one look at me and the old chemistry would come back and in her excitement maybe she'd hurl a vending machine at me. We would trash a huge section of Boston and then have a tearful conversation in the rubble where we would hash out all the reasons why we hadn't really talked since Raine died. But Sally had gotten quieter and more serious, like some Hamster family genes had kicked in or something. As for me, I'd gone through a bad year and change.

For a while there, I couldn't eat any solid food without imagining Raine's skull bursting open and pieces of his brain going into my mouth. I got so skinny and tweaked out, the Army recruiter doctors had taken one look and just laughed at the idea of militarizing me. But then the draft had been suspended for the time being, and I'd started eating food occasionally.

After dinner, we watched some of Sally and Janelle's movie. I started bouncing up and down in my seat when the movie showed Janelle stirring her coffee for two whole minutes. You shouldn't stir something for more than a few seconds unless you're baking, and even then you can usually cut the directions in half. (Gooey is good and lumpy is a sign of love.) Janelle walked down a street, stared at a tree, went to the supermarket, ate corn flakes and had a halting conversation with this other woman. Sally must have noticed the look on my face, or the fact that my fidgeting had gotten multi-dimensional, because she said it would be better with music and after editing. I said it was great, and I was just jumping up and down because I liked it so much. Uh huh, said Janelle with a little skepticism. What I didn't get was why the cat didn't talk more. If you have a movie about a talking cat, shouldn't the cat talk all the time? But Sally explained the talking cat was a metaphor, and we were supposed to see Janelle's trip to the post office through the *lens* of the talking cat.

Sally brought some friends home after her classes on the second day, because some of her classmates were curious to meet me after seeing our webmovies and hearing about me from Sally. I got confused. Sally's classmates were fans of *Thighcycle Beef* and the half dozen other movies we'd posted online, but I also got the impression they would look down on Sally if she made movies like that now. Also, Sally seemed embarrassed that they liked her "early works." One of them was named Zapp Stillman, and he was the great grandson of a famous director whom I'd never heard of. He had artful tufts of curly brown hair, giant sunglasses and a big sweatband, over a tunic and shorts. According to him, our high school movies were "kinetic but static," because I was constantly in motion but nothing ever changed, and that was "kinda Zen, really."

"I know the talking-cat movie is kind of ass, but that's why I'm in school," Sally said when we finally got a moment alone together. "To try lots of different things and, yeah, to fuck up at most of them. But I need to expand my repertoire." That made total sense to me. I'd already figured out that Sally had outgrown our dumb high school movies, and I admired her for it. Just when I was getting ready to tell Sally that I was heading back to North Carolina in a couple days, and I'd be out of her hair, she said, "Look, are you sticking around? Maybe we can fuck around on weekends, short films. We can have, like, a video tumble with new shorts going online. I'm just thinking of the ad revenue, people might actually want to buy e-books or some other cyber-poo after watching our movies. Young Urban Survivalists and shit. We appeal to that demo, hey?" I said yeah, I could totally see the Yussies watching our demented movies. So Sally figured she could make serious arty movies during the week, and dumb little action-comedies with me on weekends.

I got a job at the convenience store across Commonwealth Ave. from Boston University, not too far from where I was crashing. Walking to work, I learned to watch where I stepped, because the sidewalks had drugged-up bodies everywhere and the worst thing about stepping on one of those people wasn't the crunch underfoot or the stains on your pants cuff, it was the way they wouldn't react. Not a peep. Like they were too far gone. (Actually, the worst part was the way their blood-smeared faces reminded me of Raine, his exploding head.) Also, sometimes you would walk by a bank that was in the process of being firebombed, and chunks of flaming atrium would fly right at your head. I tried to get an explanation for the debt crisis, but it boiled down to: We owed ourselves too much for too long, until we just couldn't forgive ourselves any longer.

The next weekend, Sally and I met at the foot of one of the zillions of fancy stone bridges across the

Charles. A freeway on-ramp swooped up alongside a steep bank with colonies of shivering geese and ducks moulting next to the river's edge. Sally had a viking costume that a friend had built for the Ring Cycle a few years before, plus a giant halberd-type thing, and there was a skateboard that Sally could transform into a mythical beast in Zap!mation. I would come zooming down the freeway ramp and then go flying across the feeder lane and off the riverbank into the water. I wasn't sure about this plan, because there's a difference between comedy and just stunts. I wasn't sure what made this funny, plus what was my motivation? Sally suggested that I could be a viking warrior chasing something, but it all sounded sketchy to me. We stood around arguing, me in my horned helmet and fur vest and her in jeans and sweatshirt, for half an hour. "Shit, I get enough of this during the week," Sally said. Finally, we agreed I'd be a viking riding on the World Serpent and attempting to gather some golden apples from the World Tree. The resulting short film wasn't one of our greatest, but at least I only had a mild concussion and the halberd-whatever-it-was missed my eye socket by a good half inch.

The last thing I wanted, the first time back working on a movie with Sally in over a year, was to get all high-concept on her and drive her nuts. I knew we were just making silly, throwaway movies that would glimmer for a moment on the Internet. I just wanted to have some reason in my head why I was climbing the Harvard science building with people throwing sex toys at me. I made a list of all the reasons that somebody could be rocking at top speed through a treacherous situation:

1) Love, with some huge and fast-moving obstacle to overcome
2) Economic desperation and the promise of financial reward
3) Politics and electioneering
4) War, social upheaval, urban combat or refugeeism
5) Supernatural forces, or mental illness, or maybe family troubles

There were probably other reasons, but those were the only ones I could think of.

I was glad not to be going back down South, what with all the urban combat and people in different-colored headgear shooting at each other and that guy who played the sheriff on that sitdram getting himself torn in half just like at a tractor pull. I couldn't tell if things had gotten way worse just since I'd gone up north, or whether the news just looked worse from here, or both. But then I saw the footage of Wilmington, the water surging over the rubble, and I had to call my parents to make sure they were okay. Not like we were any safer in Boston.

Sally and I quickly realized the other film students would do almost anything we wanted, as long as we let them make superior-ass remarks about it. Once we acknowledged they were way too eminent in their artist-hood for the crap we were making, they'd work themselves into a coma and back, just for our dumb weekend movies. The first few weeks there were just half a dozen film students, then a dozen, then a couple dozen. We were up to our asses in turtlenecks! Soon we had to devise fancier and fancier set pieces to keep everyone occupied. We built a chunk of Roman coliseum in Boston Common, in an hour and a half, out of styrofoam blocks and set dressings that people hauled out of storage for us. And then we had to decide what to do with a Roman coliseum. How about some kind of vacuum-cleaner-salesman versus gladiator riff? Time travel, hand-waving, okay, go! With a vacuum cleaner/broadsword duel? Vacuum cleaner salesmen are the natural enemies of gladiators. And then the snarky film students all blogged about our movies when they got home, so all their friends reblogged it.

Apparently there's this thing called a filming permit, and the police prefer you to have it. *Oh dear, officer, we had no idea, we're actually just making a home movie here to show to our parents back home, and oh gosh, is that really a firebomb that strange dude is setting up against the wall of that shopping center?* Just mentioning firebombs got the police excited, after the recent incidents and especially with all the rumors the red bandanas were coming up North. And meanwhile everyone kept talking about how China was secretly the power propping up the Pan-Asian Ecumen and everything was all connected and we were victims of a scheme that was so complicated, the details changed every time you heard about it. Tensions climbed off the scale, and people talked of cranking up the draft again. It didn't make much sense to me, especially since all of the instability in Central Asia was hurting China worse than anybody. But that's why I leave the geopolitics to other people. I'm just the go-to guy if you want someone to ride a vacuum cleaner off the top of a styrofoam coliseum into a mosh pit of gladiators, Mormons (real Mormons, not costumes) and a confused cop.

One day when I was over at Sally's place, I saw a leader of the red bandanas being interviewed, on television: a beefy guy in his mid-twenties with a buzzcut and sideburns named Ward. They kept wanting to ask him about reports that the red bandanas were funded by some crazy trillionaire, and he kept wanting to change the subject to China, and how our government was too soft and we would soon have the tools to deal with the Chinese threat once and for all, but we wouldn't have the guts to use them. As soon as Sally saw who was on television, she turned it off and then broke the remote control against the wall.

This guy came into the half-stocked convenience store where I was working, and he wanted me to empty out the safe. He had a waxy mustache and soul patch, and he wore a poncho over a bulky football sweatshirt and knee-high socks. He was waving a shotgun that looked like someone had shot a grouse with it back in 2009, and then it had sat in a closet since then. I thought about angles of escape, up over his head or around behind the Juicy Yoo cooler, then shrugged and put up my hands. The trouble was, he couldn't get at the safe because it was keyed to my vital signs, so if my heart or breathing sped up then the safe went into total lockdown, and if my heart stopped then every alarm went dog-crazy. My boss Ramon couldn't even get any cash for legitimate purposes half the time because I'd be doing jumping jacks and thinking about whether we should stage a trolley accident or a scooter joust this weekend. I had to practice no-mind deep breathing just so my boss could grab petty cash. With this guy waving his gun at me, my heart juddered so damn hard the tumblers in the safe hugged each other for dear life. He almost gave up and left, but then he found some extra drowsy cough syrup and made me drink some of it along with a ton of Grand Marnier, with that shotgun in my face the whole time I was chugging. My heart stayed ferret-like, and I told the guy he'd have to be patient and wait for the stuff to take effect. He wanted to keep force-feeding me downers but I reminded him that if I died the safe locked up tight. He and I ended up sitting around the store a couple hours, talking about old movies and video games and stuff. Reginald loved all the cop buddy comedies of the eighties and nineties, and he could recite long sections of *Lethal Weapon* from memory. Before I even knew what I was doing, I was telling Reginald that a bunch of us made our own amateur movies in Boston Common and he should swing by this Saturday and join in. I guess it was the cough syrup, or just the fact that we'd been talking for ages and he'd put down the gun by then. Five minutes after Reginald thanked me and wandered off down the street, I took a deep breath and heard the safe un-jam itself.

"So wait. This guy came in with a shotgun and threatened you, and, and, *drugged* you, and you invited him to come make movies?" my flatmate Carrie said when I got home. Since that was a pretty complete summary of my evening, I didn't have much to say in response, except that I'd been thinking more about my character. Not my real-life character, which I didn't really know much about, but my movie character. Think about it! Harold Lloyd is the same guy in every one of his movies—a small-town innocent, maybe a little egg-headed but not street smart, with his heart on his sleeve but also full of crazy ambitions. I could be like that, except maybe more cunning and just a little loopy. Or okay, a lot loopy. Coming off the super-cold-relief formula and cognac buzz, I felt a swelling urgency that people should root for me, not just laugh at my hijinks.

Janelle, the cute film student with the rainbow dreads, agreed with me. The comic hero has to be lovable or relatable, or at least there has to be a moment of connection with the audience in between all the falling gargoyles, she said. The two of us cornered Sally, who kept trying to get us to talk to her hands. Sally was like, "I make art during the week, this weekend shit is just for fun." But Janelle and I both said it wasn't about art, just making the fun as fun as possible.

I forgot to mention about Reginald the corner-store robber, until he showed up on Saturday wearing some kind of bright red wrestling costume, or maybe those were just his regular exercise clothes. We dressed Reginald up as a cop, and a bunch of the film school kids were a motorcycle gang who'd started riding bicycles because gas was $12 a gallon, so they all overcompensated by whooping really loud and blasting heavy metal when they pedaled into town. Someone had renovated a whole section of Boston near the river to look like a little "ye olde" village, except it was really all yuppie boutiques that had been boarded up since the debt crisis. So we turned it into a small town that was trying to keep the bikers out with the help of Reginald the cop, and I got mixed up in the middle of their conflict because I had to deliver a cactus to a sick friend. Once again, my motivation was a little hazy, and it bothered me as well as Janelle. Sally had her elbow in the way of us doing any kind of love story, for some reason I could never figure. It wasn't just that she'd gotten her heart pulped with her boyfriend Raine's head. She was just dead set against goo-goo eyes. I always tried to remind her about that old saying, that a woman needs a man like a fish needs a bicycle, because what could be more romantic than a school of fish, perched on bikes at the bottom of the ocean, pedaling like wild with all their fins?

Everybody thought Reginald rocked, especially the sequence where a bunch of the bikers rode up a giant ramp we made out of an old herbal facial spa sign and flew over Reginald's head while he tried to kick-box with their wheels. Except that Reginald somehow managed to break Zapp Stillman's nose, but the other film geeks said it would just add some boxery distinction to his face. Sally asked where I found Reginald and I said I just ran into him. Reginald nearly dropped me off the Longfellow Bridge when he found out this was a volunteer gig, but I convinced him the exposure would help him to get other, paying gigs. He got pretty jazzed thinking about his roundhouse popping up all over the Internet and becoming a cult phenom. He was pretty glad he didn't actually kill me, at least for now.

Carrie kept insisting I should tell Sally the truth about Reginald, but I figured he would probably disappear soon anyway, since he made me look like long-attention-span guy by comparison. I hadn't been able to concentrate much before Raine died, but ever since I ate a piece of Raine's brain I was a human jitter.

People hit our vumble like bam bam bam. Sally thought soon we'd be more popular than we were in high school, and we sold some advertisements. People would bring us pieces of meat and shoes in return for an ad on the site sometimes. Sally got that gleam in her eye, the one she used to get when Yangar loved her. But she also kept saying how un-artistic our movies were, compared to the fancy stuff she and Janelle were doing for film school.

So Zapp Stillman was a hyper-mega rich social-ite, who didn't really notice a lot of what was going on around him, and I was his overeager manservant trying to cater to all his idiotic whims. Despite what Reginald had done to Zapp's face, he still looked delicate and sheltered, and I got to wear this great houndstooth suit that fit really well except for the arms, shoulders, knees and crotch. I practiced walking straight and butlery, which only made me more splashmanic, and then Zapp and I were supposed to go on a trip to the seaside except I had to shelter him from all the violence on the streets. Zapp hadn't read a blog or seen a newscast in years and I kept him unaware of the state of the world. So for example, we rode our two-seater bicycle past piles of comatose bodies, and I convinced Zapp it was just a group of people camping out for tickets to the Imagine Dragons reunion tour. And then a bunch of guys on scooters chased us to rip our heads off, and I told Zapp it was a friendly race. (All dialogue was big black captions, like in a proper old-school movie.) It was a cool movie with good character moments, but a ton of stuff went wrong when we were filming. Like we staged a fake riot, with a bunch of film students in ripped-up clothes pulling down bricks we'd placed strategically. Some random people wandered by and saw what was going on, and they wanted to join in and pretty soon they were tossing big chunks of wall around, and they saw Zapp and me on our dorky bicycle built for two and threw rocks at us, so the pedaling-for-dear-life sequences were hella more realistic than we'd bargained on. The camera guys had to run like stoats to keep their equipment from being smashed.

Mid-summer, Boston was all melty but people on the street sold home-made ice cream and you could ignore all the rotting smells if you thought about the river ducks. I still felt like I was about to crash everyone around me into the gritty old walls. I would forget for a second, I would bounce down the street, jumping over the people on the sidewalk and swinging on the low oak branches. And then I would have a mental image of myself, landing the wrong way, with my foot in someone's stomach, maybe someone I loved or maybe a stranger.

Some nights I couldn't sleep because every time I closed my eyes I saw Raine getting his head exploded, the chunks of skull flying apart, the brains splattering into my open mouth. This image blended together with all the ways I'd injured people by accident, or the times when I *could have* injured people if things had gone a little different. Raine's head got pulpier and more vivid each time.

Janelle and I got together and wrote a movie script, to Sally's total horror. "Okay, so what is this story about?" Janelle asked me twenty or thirty times. We sat on an abandoned swan boat in the middle of the lake in Boston Common, which kept almost capsizing as water sloshed in and out of its gullet. Once tourists had chugged around in these boats but now they just bobbed their rotting shells in and out of the algae. I didn't know what our story was about, since I didn't even know what the story was. Couldn't we take one leap at a time? But Janelle was scary patient and kept talking themes: communication, the evils of Social Darwinism, the impossibility of really knowing other people because the closer you get to them the harder it is to see the whole person. Janelle had run away from home as a kid, and lived in the attic of a bookstore cafe for years, reading every book in the stockroom and living off of abandoned scones and salads.

Nobody had known she was there until she used the store's address for her B.U. application and the acceptance letter turned up.

We settled on this O. Henry thing where a man and a woman are each trying to save each other from some horrible fate, but in the process of trying to save each other, they're putting themselves in worse danger than before. So I'm this scrappy DJ who owes money to gangsters, who could maybe be Vikings because we had some helmets and fake fur. And Janelle is a dancer who posed for some questionable photos years ago and now this sleazy guy wants to publish them and her strict family will disown her. So I decide to break in and snag the sleazy guy's hard drive, while Janelle wants to do whatever it takes to raise money to bail me out—even take on a dancer job that turns out to involve dancing on an unstable scaffolding at a construction site. And then the Vikings turn up while I'm trying to break into the sleazy guy's studio, and they want to break my legs but the sleazy guy has a protection deal with the Steampunk mafia (because we had a whole crate full of old Steampunk and Dickens Fair paraphernalia.) So we have a pitched Viking-Steampunk battle in a photography studio, while I'm trying to slip past them and grab the hard drive. And then Janelle somehow falls off her scaffolding into the middle of our fracas and I have to run around to catch her. It only took us about five hours to come up with that storyline, and by then the swan was submerged up to its neck and water slopped over the sides of its torso. We had to haul ourselves up onto the bridge without breaking our necks.

Janelle took a day off film school to help me location-scout our movie, called *Photo Finish*. We found this large art/performance space which people actually used as an art studio. She kept wanting to add more messages to the film, like about the downward spiral towards another pointless high-tech war with the entire continent of Asia, and whether Steampunk and Viking mob enforcers might have radically different attitudes to the whole concept of cultural imperialism, and this could somehow factor into their epic battle.

Reginald nearly bit her head off, trembling in his charging-bull helmet and muppet fur cloak, while she coached him on his lines. "No, come on Reggie, try it again and this time put everything you've got into the word 'maul.' You have to *feel* that word. Jesus, Rock, where did you find this guy?" She tried to choreograph the big Viking-Steampunk throwdown, even down to me throwing the big photographic backdrops in people's faces and Zapp Stillman, the Steampunk leader, hurling his brass saber pistol at a Viking and hitting the sought-after hard drive instead.

The fifth time we stopped so Janelle could micro-manage, Reginald looked ready to light the set on fire, rip several people's heads off, and then use his broadsword to make a head-kebab. I was having seismic levels of fidgetyness, to the point where I had to hug myself. Sally pulled me aside. "Jesus, what the fuck are we going to do about Janelle?" Sally torqued her elbows and claws. "She's driving me fucking bonkers, man." I didn't have many answers, except that I was worried about Reginald's inside-out fuse. Another hour went by and you could have made a milkshake on my head. It was thirty seconds' filming and then wait wait wait, ready, no hang on, wait, wait.

The tenth time we stopped, I jittered myself dizzy and stumbled into Zapp Stillman, and before he could finish saying he begged my pardon I fell and on the way down I kicked Zapp's piston-powered cyborg arm into Reginald's crotch, and Reginald fell on top of three other Vikings, so their swords jabbed into his back. He jumped up and announced that just because he'd failed to kill me the first time didn't mean he couldn't finish the job now. He grabbed a long, razor-sharp-looking hook from the studio corner and ran at me. Out of the corner of my eye, I saw Sally gesture to Janelle to get this on film for godssake. Zapp Stillman tried to get between Reginald and me, and Reginald whacked him in the face. I ducked under a big platform and kicked a cart of A/V stuff at Reginald, but he jumped over the cart without breaking his run. Several of the other Steampunks thought this was part of the movie, and tried to attack Reginald with their aetheric vaporizers, but he just cracked their heads together, so their pith hats shattered. Meanwhile I slid out the other end of the platform and climbed the curtain rope. The rope was on a pully, so Reginald started pulling and the rope went down as the curtain went up. I had to climb at top speed to stay at the same altitude. Reginald kept pulling the rope with one hand and threw his spike-hook with the other, but I caught the hook and dug it into the curtain, then let go of the rope and swung on the hook across to the other side of the curtain, which tore as I went, so I landed on the ground across the room. A random Viking swung at my head and I barely ducked in time, then I saw a bucket full of water (which was supposed to be photographic solution) and I dumped it on Reginald's head. His helmet's horns stabbed through the bucket so he couldn't get it off, and he started grabbing anyone who got in his way, even other Vikings, and tossing them.

At first I screened the sirens out, because you heard sirens all the time, but I heard more and more, fire sirens as well as cop. Peal after peal, like church bells. I leaned out the window to see what was going on and then Reginald was at my ear, trying to push me out. He'd gotten the helmet and bucket off, and he had one hand under my armpit and the other on my belt. It was probably twenty feet down. I could see flames in the distance, and tongues of smoke from a few other places. I tried to tell Reginald I hadn't meant to hurt him, but he just pushed harder. The window frame gave way and we both tumbled. I twisted my body so Reginald hit the ground first and I landed on top of him.

I couldn't see anything but I smelled smoke worse than ever. My crotch felt broken, my feet felt broken. I forced my eyes open but everything had a double image. Sally had the door to the studio building open nearby and was yelling for me to get my ass inside. I limped to my feet and juddered in, then Sally locked the door behind me. Through the window I watched Reginald try to raise himself up.

"Example of the sort of human garbage they tolerate up here," a voice said. It sounded sort of like Ricky Artesian, from back home, but wasn't. I found a window with a view of the guy, who was a little smaller than Ricky and had tufty black hair. He dressed like Ricky and had the same red bandana. So did the half dozen or so guys behind him. The guy talked for half an hour about Reginald, who kept trying to get to his feet but couldn't quite manage it. Reginald had the bad luck to be the only guy nearby who looked like a junkie and couldn't run for his life. I wanted to go out and help him, but I could barely move and Sally half-supported, half-restrained me. Sally wanted to stop watching when they got into it with the crowbars, but this was my fault, sort of, and I had to see it play out. They didn't torch him until they ran out of bones. I hoped he would black out, but he kept screaming the whole time, on fire. Maybe some people can black out and scream at the same time? I sure hoped so.

Rock Manning Goes for Broke

So at this point, you're wondering what happened to *Photo Finish*. It was our most popular vumble entry yet, even though we only filmed about half the scenes Janelle had scripted, and what we recorded didn't have that much in common with her and my storyline. Sally and some of the others did a fantastic job tweaking it with Zap!mation, to the point where that studio looked like twenty different places. With the red bandanas turning up all over the country and imposing mob rule, everyone was primed for people in silly costumes whacking each other. It turns out when everything is turning into bloody shit, that's when people need Vikings against Steampunks more than ever. Who knew?

The police tried to stop the red bandanas at first, but then the President went on television and said they were an official militia, like in the Constitution, because we were losing our grip, as a nation. It was probably the Pan-Asiatic Ecumen's fault, but nobody knew for sure.

Two days later, Sally said I had to get out of the house and breathe, because too many people were staying indoors all the time and we had a duty to show we weren't scared. I crutch-hopped my way down the empty street, as Sally ran rings around me for a change. I was glad I didn't have to step over junkies anymore, even though I worried about what had happened to all of them. Sally said prison camps, or bonfires, or just underground hideouts.

All of the film students cheered for me! Even the ones who'd high-backed me when I first showed up in town. Maybe because I'd become a casualty of art, or maybe because the new movie had gotten mad hits. Either way, people wanted to carry me around and pour stuff down my throat, and everyone signed my osteogenic body-sheath. We were promoting creative anarchy and that made us super important radical artists, and hey, we should take it to the next level somehow. I thought if they wanted to promote anarchy, maybe we could find one of the camps, in Medford or Malden, where the red-hanky guys had rounded up the homeless people and undesirables, and set them all free. We could film it. We could put Napoleon hats on all of them and turn them loose. It would look cool, sort of like the final episode of *The Prisoner*. Everybody liked that idea, and they were all up for doing it, but not on a day when they had classes. The film students kept adding more and more layers to the plan. We would dress as farm animals, and there would be a huge round clock which we'd roll down hill to cause a distraction, and maybe we could time the attack to coincide with a joint lunar/solar eclipse so the lack of both moon and sun would sensory-deprive everyone. They jumped up and down with excitement, but I finally realized they were making the plans fancier and fancier because they didn't want to have to follow through. That was fine with me because I was only half serious about the camp liberation idea too.

"Most of those guys, you just tell them where to stand and what to do, and they're happy. Don't make them think too hard," Sally told me afterwards. Our movies had built her into a queen bee. She wanted to walk me home, but the sun sagged and I didn't want her caught out after dark. I ran into a couple of red-bandana groups on my way home, but I told them I was a friend of Ricky Artesian's and they practically saluted. The second group insisted on escorting me home. Film students and red bandanas, both whooping at me, all in one day!

Soon enough I was healed enough to go back to work at the convenience store, where I kept seeing bone-crushed Reginald on fire whenever I looked at the lighters. Nowadays, I saw both Raine and Reginald in my dreams, unless I watched some Buster Keaton right before bedtime.

Some of Carrie's friends were planning a giant protest against the red bandanas and the economic policies and the move to expand the war, and the crazy weapon projects like that sonic cannon that people claimed would make a whole city shake itself to pieces from a distance. I was leery because, duh, the last time I'd gone to a protest I'd wound up covered in slippery bodies, choking on a piece of my friend's brain.

I started hoping my body wouldn't heal too quickly, because once it did they would expect me to create more serious mayhem, and just the thought of it made me start to shamblequake. Sally texted me saying it was time to do some more mad slapstick, and I texted back that we really needed to talk.

I have a perfect recall of my meeting with Sally, maybe cause it was the last time we ever spoke to each other.

We met in the middle of the Mass Avenue bridge, with faded paintwork measuring the bridge's span in "Smoots," the height of some long-ago MIT student whose classmates had rolled him across the bridge. On either side of us, the river swelled with gray bracken and flecks of brown foam, and in front of us, the jagged Boston sky-line. The John Hancock Tower's windows had all started falling out and hitting people on the head, so they'd condemned the whole building and only gotten halfway through demolishing it, and now it looked like a shiny blue-green zig-zag climbing to a single razor point. We watched the water churn a while. The wind battered us.

Sally was gushing about my chemistry with Zapp Stillman, and how much people liked seeing the two of us interact, and maybe we could do a few more clips featuring the two of us. Gang boss and lieutenant, an inept leather daddy and his boy, boxer and trainer, rock star and manager, super-heroes. The possibilities were endless, almost like having Raine back. For a moment I wondered if Sally had a thing for Zapp's gangly ass.

"That's why I wanted to talk to you," I said once I could break in. "I need to take a break from making movies. I was thinking of going back to North Carolina." I tried to explain how I kept seeing Raine and Reginald whenever I closed my eyes lately, but Sally grabbed my scruff and pushed me halfway over the edge of the bridge. My pants fell down and the wind whipped through my boxer shorts. My ass was in space.

"You asshole," Sally said. "What the fuck is wrong with you? Every time I think I can rely on

you. What the fuck? I was going to be a real director. I was doing great in film school, making serious
movies. And then you turned up and sucked me
back into spending all my time making these dumb
comedies instead. And now you're just going to
leave? What? The? Fuck?" She shook me with each
word. My shirt tore around the armpits. I could feel
my feet, somewhere far away, trampling my pants.

"I'm sorry. I'm so sorry." I looked up into her
bugged out eyes. "I just can't. I can't deal. Jesus,
you're my best friend no matter how long I live,
but I'm a poison time bomb, you don't want to be
around me, I'll just hurt you, I'm so sorry."

She hauled me off the edge and dumped me
on my feet. "What the fuck are you talking about,
Rock? I love you, but you're an idiot. Just listen
to me, okay. You're not some kind of destructive
engine. You are good for exactly one thing, and one
thing only, and that's turning people's brains off
for a few minutes. You should stick to that. And
another thing, did you ever stop to think about
what I'm getting out of doing these movies with

you? Did you? I mean, jeez. The world we live in now, the only time things make sense is when I'm coming up with bigger and crazier disasters to put on film. I finally decided, slapstick is the new realism. And I can't do it without you. Do you understand what I'm saying?"

"Yeah, but..." I took a breath and pulled up my pants. The snap had broken, so I had to hold them together with one hand, and that limited my gesture menu a lot. "I keep feeling like I'm going to hurt somebody. I feel like people keep getting hurt around me, and maybe it's my fault somehow. Like what happened with Reginald. And Raine, before that."

"Jesus, this pisses me off. My boyfriend dies, but it's still all about you. What is up with that?"

The bridge rumbled, and I worried the supports had eroded or someone had sabotaged them. I tried to get Sally's attention, but she was still talking about how dumb I was. I grabbed her arm with my free hand and pulled her towards land. She jerked free and said she didn't want to go with me, she was sick of my crap, let go.

"Listen, listen! Something's wrong," I said. I pulled her the other way, towards Boston. By now the bridge was definitely vibrating in a weird way. I could feel it in my teeth. I ran as fast as I could without letting go of my pants-clasp. The bridge felt like it was going to collapse any second. We made it to land, but the sidewalks had the same problem as the bridge. The rumbling got louder and felt like it was coming from inside me.

"What the fuck is going on?" Sally shouted. I raised my hands. By now I was seeing funny, like there were one and a half of her. My teeth clattered. My stomach cramped up. And most of all my ears were full, they hurt like murder. I had earaches like someone had jammed sticks into my ear canals, it hurt all the way down my throat.

The last words Sally ever said to me were, "What the hell, we need to get inside—"

The pressure inside my ears built up and then it spiked, like the sticks in my ears had jammed all the way in and twisted like a corkscrew. I can't really describe the pain. People have written tons of poems about it, but mostly they use it as something to compare any other kind of pain with. Two giant hands smacked me in the head, at the same time as a massive force tried to push its way out from the inside of my skull. I staggered and fell over, nearly blacked out.

Blood burst out of Sally's ears at the same time as I felt something splash on my shirt. I tried to say something like, What the fuck just happened, or Shit I dropped my pants again, but nothing came out. No, I was doing all the right things to make a sound, but nothing. I couldn't hear birds or street sounds. I couldn't hear anything. Sally was moving her mouth too, but she had the same panic in her eyes as I felt. I sat down on the ground, impact but no noise, like we were in outer space.

Sally was still trying to talk, tears coming down her cheeks. I gestured that I couldn't hear her. She grabbed her phone and fumbled with the buttons. A second later, my phone vibrated. A text message: "wtf im deaf." I texted back: "me 2." She wrote: "we need help."

She hauled me to my feet and found a safety pin in her bag, for my stupid pants. Then we rushed down Mass Ave, looking for someone who could call an ambulance. I still felt jumpy crossing the streets without being able to hear cars or other vehicles coming up behind me. Plus I kept turning to look over my shoulder in case someone ran up behind me. We found a guy up near Commonwealth Ave, but we could see from a distance he was clutching his ears and crying. Same with the half a dozen young people we saw near the boarded-up Urban Outfitters at Mass Ave and Newbury. They all had blood on their shoulders and were texting each other or using pidgin sign language. They tried to plead for our help with their hands, until they realized we had the same problem.

Everywhere we went, newly deaf people wigged out. Sally texted me that we needed to get off the streets, this was going to get ugly. I knew what she meant. Carrie texted me that she'd gone deaf and I told her to get indoors. Sally and I found bikes and rode back to her house as fast as we could, not stopping for traffic lights or any of the people who tried to flag us down.

Janelle kissed her knees on the sofa, her back heaving. The television showed people, all over the world, with bloody ears. Somewhere an airplane had crashed, and somewhere else a power plant had blown up. There was no newscaster, just words scrolling across the screen. "THE SITUATION IS UNDER CONTROL. STAY TUNED FOR UPDATES. DO NOT GO OUTDOORS. TOTAL HEARING LOSS APPEARS TO BE WORLDWIDE. DO NOT GO OUTDOORS. AUTHORITIES HAVE NO EXPLANATION. STAY INSIDE." We went on the Internet and read everything we could find. If anyone on the planet could still hear, there was no sign. Every blog, every email group, was full of people freaking out. Only the people who had already been part of the Deaf community stayed calm, and they posted teach-yourself-sign-language videos. I knew right away I would never have the patience to learn sign language.

It only took a few hours for the conspiracy theories to start spinning. The Pan-Asian Ecumen had tested out some weapon. Or the U.S. had. A weapon test had gone wrong, or maybe it had gone right. Maybe something had happened with that sonic cannon we'd kept hearing was going to win the war that everyone craved, or maybe it was a false flag by the anti-war protestors, or maybe both. Why not both? Really, it could be anything.

For now, all you could see on television was swarming crowd scenes that looked identical no matter which city-name they stuck at the bottom of the screen. People knocking into each other and everything else, a perpetual motion machine that couldn't move. Close-ups of faces in Shanghai and Cleveland, pushed beyond scowls, into some new facial expression that we had yet to put a name to. We had thought we were getting stronger, cleaner, rejecting every confusing piece of ourselves while we prepared to defeat everyone who had ever tried to undermine our national will, but maybe we had just misdirected ourselves. Most of these big production numbers just reminded me of the protest where Raine's head exploded in front of me, so I changed the channel or walked away whenever they came on.

Day two or three, I got fed up and decided to go to work. By then, we were running out of stuff at Sally's house, and Janelle and even Sally were starting to get on my nerves. They could feel the vibrations from my fidgeting and the impact when I broke something of theirs, even when they couldn't see me. And I could feel their grief like a blanket all around me. My thumbs got sore from text-messaging Sally when she was sitting right next to me. I could have just as much of a conversation from long distance. Sally didn't want me to go out because the television was still full of people thrashing each other, but I said I'd be careful.

I didn't even know if the convenience store still existed, and nobody had told me to come in to work. But nobody had told me not to, either. And this could be my contribution to society's continued existence, selling spam and condoms to people. I passed plenty of looted stores on my way down Commonwealth, and people were lighting all sorts of things on fire that were probably terrible for the environment. But when I got to the Store 24, it was still there and in one piece. I opened it up. It occurred to me that people would have a hard time asking me how much things cost. So I got out the pricing gun and went around making sure every single item in the store had an individual price sticker, even down to the 37-cent instant noodles. After that, I had to learn how to stay alert, because the little new-customer bell was no more use to me. An hour or two went by, more boring than anything I'd ever experienced before.

"thk gd yr here," said the message on the guy's cell phone, waved in my face. I nodded and he pulled it away to thumb some more. "didnt want 2 loot." I nodded. "but no stores open." I nodded. Then he went and filled his basket with canned goods, and brought it back. I rung him up, and he shook my hand with both hands. He looked like a college professor, fiftyish, white, wearing plaid and stripes and tweed, so he wasn't a professor of fashion design. He saluted, like I was a colonel, then left.

Word spread, and more people came to the store. The shelves got emptier, and I pulled out stuff from the back room. We were going to run out of goods, and I didn't know if any more was coming. People, mostly middle class, thanked me for saving them from being looters. People are funny. I wish I'd had the URL of our vumble handy. I think a lot of those people would have looked at whatever I wanted to show them.

A TV news crew came to "interview" me. Mostly they filmed me serving customers and clowning around. I wrote our URL on a piece of paper and held it up to the camera. Sally said the news channel showed me twice an hour for a day or two, with a scrolling banner saying "LIFE RETURNS TO NORMAL." My boss text-messaged me and said he'd stop by to empty the safe and register.

Nobody robbed me, even after I was on television, because there were plenty of abandoned stores to rob.

The non-news channels went back to showing regular stuff, except with Closed Captions for everybody. But all the words at the bottom of the screen made all the old sitcoms look like French movies, so I kept waiting for Jennifer Aniston to smoke or commit incest.

Sally emailed her film-geek crew, including Zapp, about our next shoot. Who knew if they were even going to have classes any time soon? She bopped around a little more, bouncing dumb ideas off me, and once or twice she seemed to laugh. I still caught her staring into space or crying into the can of liverwurst I brought home from the store.

3.

It's actually funnier without laughter

People tossed around words like "collapse of civilization" and "post-apocalyptic," but really everything was the same mess as always. Only without any soundtrack, and with a "militia" of guys in red bandanas swarming around killing everyone who got in their way. But civilization, you know, has always been a relative thing. It rises, it falls, who can keep track?

So now, sneaking up on people was suddenly way easier—but so was getting snuck up on. The fear of somebody creeping up behind me and cutting my throat was the only thing that kept me from being bored all the time. I always thought noise was boring, but silence bored me even worse. And if you walked up behind someone, especially a member of the red-bandana militia who were keeping order on our streets, you had to be very careful how you caught their attention. You did not want a red bandana to think you were sneaking up on them. And often, you'd find a whole street of stores that were there yesterday were just burned-out husks today, or bodies piled in an odd assortment, like corpse origami.

I found myself sniffing the air a lot, for danger or just for amusement. If anyone had still been able to hear, they probably would have been doubled up laughing, because we were all going around sniffing and grunting and mumbling in funny voices, as soon as we had no clue how ridiculous we sounded.

Almost every corner seemed to have red bandanas standing on it, looking bored and desperate for someone to fuck with them.

But meanwhile, I was Entertainer Explainer's New Talent of the Month, because I'd managed to avoid getting murdered in an amusing fashion, and the video had gone mega-viral. I was seeing my own face on shirts and on people's phablets more and more often. Sally and I were suddenly kind of famous and we had to clear out our freezer to make room for all the meat and casseroles and stuff that people kept bringing over. Sally thought our dumb web movies were the ideal thing for people to watch now, because they were the wacky escape from reality, and they had no dialogue or sound effects for anyone to miss out on. "it's actually funnier without any laughter," Sally texted me from three feet away.

Everybody was bracing themselves for the next thing. We still believed in money, kinda-sorta, even after a ton of people had lost their savings and investments in the big default spiral. We didn't not believe in money, let's put it that way. We still had electricity and cellphone service and internet, even though many parts of the country were on-again, off-again. The red bandanas and the rump government needed a cellular network as bad as the rest of us, because they needed to be able to organize, the conventional wisdom said, so until they figured out how to have a dedicated network and their own power sources, they would make sure it kept running for everyone. We hoped, anyway.

Sally and I spent hours arguing about what sort of movie we should make next. All of my ideas were too complicated or high-concept for her. I wanted to do a movie about someone who tries to be a gangster but he's too nice, like he runs a protection racket but never collects any money from people. Or he sells drugs but only super harmless ones. So the other gangsters get mad at him, and everyone has to help him pretend to be a real gangster. And he does such a good job he becomes the head gangster, and then he's in real trouble. Or something. Anyway, Sally said that was too complicated for people right now, we had to shoot for self-explanatory. Some of the film geeks wanted us to make a movie *about* the fact that everyone was deaf, but that seemed like the opposite of escapism to me—which I guess would be trappism, or maybe claustrophilia. More and more often, people had these debates partly in sign language, and I couldn't follow what they were saying.

Sally was all about recapturing the Vikings-and-Steampunk glory, like maybe this time we could have Amish cyborgs, with hand-crafted wooden implants. I was like, Amish cyborgs aren't high concept? I was happy to keep debating this stuff forever, because I didn't actually want to make another movie. Whatever part of me that had let me turn calamity into comedy had withered when I fell out of a window on top of Reginald, and watched him die on fire.

Every time I looked, there seemed to be more red bandanas around, and I still saw them beating up subversives and hauling them away to the camps outside the city. All the people on television and my phone looked tooth-spitting angry when they even thought about anyone making trouble for these hard-working men and women (but mostly men) who were sacrificing *so much* to make us all safer in this dangerous time. I would glance at my phone to see the weather, and there would be a video of someone dressed in an authority-figure costume, looking outraged, and then the words would appear, in block capitals, like "HOW DARE YOU HAVE YOU NO SHAME," and then maybe scary video of a blurry figure in dark clothes leering at a group of red bandanas while rose-tinted flames consumed everything in the background. Even with everything I knew about Ricky and his friends, I always wanted to find the nearest red bandana and find some way to apologize for all my hurtful thoughts— like I was always groveling inside my own head for a moment after looking at my phone, until I snapped back to reality.

Snow fell. Then hail, then sleet, and then snow again. Things felt dark, even during the day, and I felt like my sight, smell and touch were going the way of my hearing. Only my taste burned as strong as ever. Everything was salty, salty, salty. You could slip and break your leg in a ditch and nobody would know you were there for days and days. This was going to be a long winter.

I had the same dream night after night, for a week or two. I was in a swan boat with Sally, in Boston Common, and everything smelled gray and brown. The water swhooshed and the ducks complained. The air, the few cars, our breathing, all had their own music. Our boat didn't need to go anywhere special, but Sally beat the water with an oar anyway. She cursed the stupid water, looked over and smiled at me, and then went back to hitting and cursing.

"What did the water do to you?" I asked Sally.

"It's not the water, it's everything. It all needs its ass kicked. Actually, the water pisses me off because it keeps running away from me. If it would just sit still, I would go easy on it."

"Look, Sally, I know you said I shouldn't blame myself. For what happened to Raine and all. But it keeps happening, over and over, and when something happens more than twice, chances are it's my fault, right?"

Sally stopped scaring the ducks and touched my arm. She had amazing lightness sometimes. "There's plenty of blame to go around, scooter. You can have your share, don't worry, and I'll have mine. We'll make a party of divvying it up."

The sky got dark purple all at once, like it does sometimes. "I just don't want to let you down any more. And I can see another shitfuck coming, bigger than the others. I'm scared I can't keep being the funny falling-down guy any longer, I feel as though I swallowed a statue and it's statue-fying me from the inside out."

Now the sky was all the way dark.

"Well, if it gets to be too much for you, you know what you can always do, don't you?" Sally took both my shoulders in her hands as things got darker and darker, and said, "What you do is—" And that's where I always woke up.

"ROCK MANNING, WE NEED YOU."

I stared up at the giant scrolling light-up banner over Out Of Town News in Harvard Square. I blinked the snow away and looked a second time. It still looked like my name up there. Okay, so this was it, the thing my school therapist had warned me about back in fifth grade. I was going narcissistophrenic and starting to imagine that toasters and people on the television were talking to me or about me. It was probably way too late to start taking pills now.

But then a guy I had met at one of our movie shoots saw it too, tugging on my sleeve and pointing at the scrolling words. So unless he and I were both hallucinating the same way, it really did say my name up there.

A bus zipped past, now that they'd gotten a few buses running again. The big flashing screen on the front didn't say, "WARNING. BUS WILL RUN YOU OVER. GET OUT OF THE WAY" as usual. Instead, it said, "ROCK MANNING, YOU CAN MAKE A CONTRIBUTION TO REBUILDING

SOCIETY." I grabbed the guy, whose name was Scottie or Thor or something, and pointed at the bus for more independent confirmation that I wasn't losing it. He poked me back and pointed at a big screen in the display window of Cardullos, which now read, "ROCK MANNING, COME JOIN US." I grabbed my cell phone, and it had a new text message, much the same as the ones I was seeing everywhere. I almost threw my phone away.

Instead I ran towards the river, trying to out-run the words. Over the past few months since the event everyone was calling the Big Boom, I'd seen the screens going up in more and more places, and now all of a sudden they were all talking to me personally. Computer screens on display at the big business store, the sign that normally announced the specials at the Mongolian buffet place—even the little screen that someone had attached to their golden retriever's collar, that would let you know when the dog was barking. They were calling me out. I got to the river, and ran across the big old stone bridge. In the murky river water, the letters floated, projected from somewhere in the depths: "WHY ARE YOU RUNNING? WE THOUGHT YOU'D BE FLATTERED."

When I got to the other side of the bridge, Ricky Artesian was waiting for me. He was wearing a suit and instead of the red bandana, he had a red hand-kerchief in his breast pocket, but otherwise he was the same old Ricky, from high school. He held up a big piece of paper:

"Relax, pal. We just need your help, the same way we needed you once before. Except this time we're going to make sure it goes right."

Ricky had a couple other guys in suits behind him, also clearly red-bandana honchos. I thought about jumping off the bridge. The river had defrosted but still looked chilly. I looked over the edge of the bridge again, tossed a mental coin and jumped.

The loose boat was right where I thought it was. It had drifted downriver from the Harvard boathouse, and I landed in the stern without cap-sizing it all the way. I righted the boat and found the oars. Someone had either forgotten to chain it up, or vandalized the chain. Then I slotted the oars into their nooks and started to row. I'd never sculled before, but how hard could it be?

After half an hour of rowing as hard as I could, and going in the same circle over and over, while Ricky watched from overhead, I wondered if I'd made a mistake, plus this all reminded me way too much of my recurring swan-boat dream. I texted Sally that I was in a boat trying to escape and didn't know how to row. She Googled row-ing. She said I needed to straighten out and row the same amount with both oars, and then maybe I'd stop going in circles. Also, go with the current. Meanwhile, Ricky and his friends were grabbing a big scary-looking hook. I tried to figure out what the current was. It took me way too long to find a drifting leaf, and figure I should go the same way as it. So I tried to row that way, but the boat kept veering and swerving. Then I saw a bench right in front of me that looked like someone was supposed to sit facing the other way, and I realized that was probably where the coxswain sat. Which was the rear of the boat, right? So maybe part of the problem was that I was sitting backwards. I got myself all turned around, but I lost my grip on one of the oars and it floated away, much faster than my boat had gone so far. At this point, the hook snagged my boat, and a moment later I was a landlubber again.

"Hey Rock," Ricky said. I was up to about ten percent accuracy with my lipreading. He held out his hand and I took it out of reflex.

We all went for burgers at this little ancient diner nearby, which had survived everything without changing its greasy ways. I admired that. It even still had the little jukebox at each table, and the red checkered vinyl tablecloth with stray burn marks from when you could still smoke indoors. Ricky smoked, because who was going to tell him not to?

"i think it's great you're still doing the same thing as in high school," Ricky's laptop screen said.

He swiveled it around and typed some more, then turned it back. Now it said: "you found something that worked for you, and you stuck with it. that's kool." I nodded. If Ricky had been talking instead of typing, he probably would have made this stuff sound like compliments. He typed some more: "you know i always liked you." The other two guys didn't try to say anything, or even read what Ricky was typing, they just ate their burgers and stared out the window at the handful of students who were crawling back to Harvard.

I didn't try to contribute to the conversation either, I just read whatever Ricky typed at me. He hadn't touched his burger yet. He told me about how he'd moved up in the world since Carolina, and now he was working for some pretty juiced-up people in government, and everything was really under control. You would be surprised, he said, at how under control everything really was.

I nodded and half-smiled, to show that I knew what he meant, but really I didn't think I would be that surprised.

Rock Manning Goes for Broke

I thought about the oar that had gotten away from me, floating downriver towards freedom, as fast as it could go. Where would it end up?

Ricky said I shouldn't worry about a repeat of what happened last time. We were both older and more experienced, and he'd gotten smarter since then. But the thing was, he said, people were still in shock. Almost like little children, right now. And they needed their cartoony entertainment to keep their minds off things. So here was the deal: he would get us resources, like you wouldn't imagine, like our wildest dreams were this tablecloth and the actuality was up there on the ceiling. And in return, we would just portray authority in a kind way. Nothing too heavy, like people wearing the bandana or any army uniforms. Just occasionally we see that the militia and Army are trustworthy, and the people in charge have your best interests, etc. etc. etc. Most of the time, we'd have a free hand.

I had to get up and go wash my hands, so I could type on Ricky's laptop. I didn't want to get his keyboard greasy. Then it took me a minute to hunt and peck: "sally wont go for it she thinks you killed her boyfriend which duh you did."

I swiveled it around before I could think twice about what I'd just typed.

Ricky's eyes narrowed. He looked up at me and for a moment he was the legbreaker again. I thought he was going to lunge across the booth and throttle me. Then he typed: "the robot guy?" I nodded. "that was a situation. its complicated, and many people were to blame."

I tried really really hard not to have any expression on my face, as if it didn't matter to me one way or the other. I ran out of hamburger, so I ate my fries slow, skinning them and then nibbling at the mashed potatoes inside. Everything smelled meaty.

"tell u what, just dont tell sally im involved," Ricky typed. "just tell her the government wants 2 support your work."

It was easy for me to agree to that, because I knew my face was a giant emoji as far as Sally was concerned, and she would know within seconds that I was hiding something.

Ricky didn't threaten to break parts of us if we didn't go along with his plan, but he didn't need to, and he only made some gauzy promises about payment. He did say he could get me some rowing lessons. Then he said he'd be in touch again soon, and he and his goons left me sitting alone in a booth staring at grease stains on a plate.

Outside, a half-dozen people were gathering on stone benches in front of a Deaf woman who was teaching with a mixture of slow, careful sign language and big posters. This group called the Kind Hands had developed some new curriculum and were mass-producing books and posters, with a heavy emphasis on empowerment and self-esteem. Across the street, two rank-and-file red bandanas studied this group, clearly trying to figure out if it was a subversive gathering, which was one of those questions that could easily fall into some pretty deep philosophical quicksand. The red bandanas watched as the woman, who had Asian features and a hat with a red pom-pom, taught people how to say "are you hungry" and "it's snowing again" in sign language, and the bandanas looked down at their phones, because this was boring.

But then just as I was half a block away, the woman unveiled a poster-sized card for how to sign "I can take care of myself." The two red bandanas looked at each other, and then they walked across the street with their clubs raised.

I searched for two hours without finding Sally. I almost texted her, but I had a bad feeling about my cell phone. When I finally tracked her down, she was bossing a group of film students building a giant ramp that looked as if they were going to roll a mail cart into a snowbank. She saw me and then turned away, to watch her pals slamming boards together. I nudged her, but she just ignored me. I remembered she'd said something about this movie they wanted to make about a guy who works in the mailroom and discovers a hidden doorway that leads to Hell's interoffice mail system, and he has to deliver a bunch of letters to demons before he can get out. High fuckin concept. Anyway, she was pissed that I'd been blowing her off for weeks, so now I couldn't get her attention.

Finally, I wrote just the name "ricky a" on my cell and shoved it in front of her, without pressing send. Her eyes widened and she made to text me back, but I stopped her. I grabbed a pad and a pen and wrote down the whole story for her, including the signs in Harvard Square. She shook her head a lot, then bit her lip. She thought I was exaggerating, but the guy who'd seen the signs showed up and confirmed that part, scribbling but also signing with his hands.

"We're so small time," she wrote in neat cursive under my scrawls. "Why would Ricky care?"

Under that, I wrote: "1. He remembers us from hi skool, unfinished biz. 2. He likes us and wants to own us. 3. He hates us and wants to destroy us. 4. those guys are scared of losing their grip & they think we can help."

A cold wind blew, and I'd gotten kind of wet trying to escape in a boat, plus the sun was going down, so I started to shiver out there on the lawn in front of BU. Some students were straggling back in, just like at Harvard, and they stared at the set, abandoned half-finished against one wall. Sally gestured for her gang to get the ramp to Hell's mail-room back into storage.

We piled ourselves into the back of the equipment van, with Zapp Stillman driving, and headed for the Turnpike, because the sooner we got out of town the better. We got about half a mile, before we hit the first checkpoint. Soldiers with big dragonfly helmets stood in front of humvees, blocking off most of the lanes of Storrow Drive, and between the soldiers and the swiveling cameras on stalks, there was no way you would get past their barricades. They were checking everybody coming in and out of the city, and 100 yards past them stood an exoskeleton thingy, or a mech, with thighs like Buicks and feet like dumpsters. I couldn't really see its top half from my hiding place in the back of the van, but I imagined piston elbows and some kind of skull face. The kind of people who built a mech like this would not be able to resist having a skull face, to save their lives. My brother Holman had probably piloted one of these things, in Central Asia or Central Eurasia, someplace Central. The pilots of these things had a high rate of going A.U.T.U., because of all the neural strain. This one wasn't moving, but it was cranked up and operational because you could see the ground shivering around it, and there were fresh kills nearby. Cars still smoking, a few unlucky bodies.

I thought of the smirk on Ricky's face as he'd typed that everything was under control.

Our van turned onto a side street as fast as possible, and we swerved back towards B.U. By the time we got back there, Janelle had found some posts on an underground forum, about the cordoning off of several major cities. This was part of a sweep to round up certain radical elements that threatened the shaky order: you had the red bandanas inside the cities, and the army outside.

We were still in the van, parked on a side street just off Dummer Street, sheltered by a giant sad oak that leaned almost to the ground on one side. You could put a tire swing on that oak and swing underground and maybe there would be mole people. Mole people would be awesome, especially if they had their own dance routine, which I just figured they probably would because what else would you be doing stuck underground all the time?

I wasn't sure if we should get out of the van, or if someone could spot us, but Sally went ahead and climbed out, and Janelle followed. I got out and stood on the sidewalk, shrugging in a sad ragdoll way. Sally stomped her foot and gritted her teeth. She tried some sign language on me, and I got the gist that she was saying we were trapped, every way out of the city would be the same thing. I just looked at her, waiting for her to say what we were going to do, and she looked weary but also pissed. This thing of not talking meant you really had to watch people, and maybe you could see people more clearly when you couldn't hear them.

I studied Sally. She had the twitch in her forearms that usually meant she was about to throw something. She had the neck tendon that meant she was about to yell at someone, if yelling were still a thing that happened. Her mouse-brown hair was a beautiful mess bursting free of her scrunchie, her face so furious it circled back around to calm. Biting her tongue, the better to spit blood.

She wrote on her phone: "the army outside + red bandanas inside. occupation. city is screwed. we r screwed. trapped." She erased it without hitting send.

I took the phone and wrote: "red bandanas + army = opportunity."

She just stared at me. I didn't even know what I had in mind yet. This was the part of the conversation where I would normally start spitballing, and suggesting that we get a hundred people in koala costumes and send them running down the street while someone else dropped hallucinogenic water balloons from a hang glider. Or something. But I couldn't spitball as fast with my thumbs. I paused and thought about Ricky, and the other bandanas I'd met, and how they were so desperate to be loved as well as feared that they were even willing to ask someone like me for help with representing. I thought about Holman, and how much he looked down on civilians, even before he got the A.N.V.I.L. socket in his skull. I thought about how Ricky and his guys had engineered a clusterfuck at that peace protest, making the cops think the protestors were shooting at them, so the cops shot back. I thought about how the bandanas weren't leaving the city, and the army wasn't coming in.

"i think I have a bad idea," I wrote.

All my life, there had been a giant empty space, a huge existential void, that had needed to be filled by something, and I had never realized that that thing was the Oscar Mayer Wienermobile, with its sleek red hot-dog battering ram surrounded by a metal bun. It was like the Space Battleship Yamato made of bread and pork, made of metal. This MIT student named Matt had been souping it up, with a high-performance electric engine and all-terrain wheels, just saving it for the right occasion. And somehow, Janelle had convinced Matt that our little adventure was it. The tires were the perfect mud color to match the lower part of the chassis, which Matt had rescued from a scrapyard in Burlington. The chassis had a tip as red and round as a clown's nose, on either side of the long, sleek body. This baby had cris-crossed the country before I was born, proclaiming the pure love of Ballpark Franks to anyone with half an eye. Just staring at this beauty made me hungry in my soul.

All around us, Sally's film-student minions were doing engine checks and sewing parachutes and painting faces onto boomerangs and inflating sex-dolls and making pies for the pie-throwing machine. The usual, in other words. I felt an emotion I'd never felt before in my life, lodged down where I always pictured my spine and my colon shaking hands, and I didn't know how to label it at first. Sort of like excitement, sort of like regret—but this feeling wasn't either of those things. I finally realized: I was afraid. People had told me about fear, but I had never quite believed it existed in real life. I watched Zapp Stillman blowing up a blow-up doll, and something wobbled inside me. I had felt guilt and self-loathing, especially after Reginald, but now I felt worry-fear. Zapp saw me looking at him, and gave me a cocky little nod. I nodded back.

Sally was busy studying a big road map with Janelle, charting the escape route and where we were all going to rendezvous if we made it out of town. Sally had taken my vague arm-wheeling notion and turned it into an actual plan, which would let us escape to the Concorde Turnpike and make for Walden Pond, that place where Henry David Thoreau had built a comedy waterslide 200 years ago. And then maybe head West. Find a secluded place to wait things out. Sally handed her magic marker off to Janelle, and came over to stand with me.

"What changed your mind," she wrote in ball-point on a pad, "about doing more stunts? You were ready to quit, before."

I took the pad and pen. Chewed the cap. Wrote: "Ricky won't leave us alone. We gotta blow town and this is the only way. Plus this is different than just making another weird movie. If this works, maybe we ruin the red bandanas' day. Maybe we ruin their whole week, even. PAYBACK." That last word, I underlined three times. Sally took the pen back from me and drew little stars and hearts and rainbows and smiley faces, until this was the most decorated "PAYBACK" you've ever seen.

One of our lookouts shone a flashlight, and Janelle nodded, and Sally and I got stuffed into a little cubby under the floorboards, with no light and almost no air, with all the cameras and filming equipment on top of us. We were scrunched together, so her knee was in my face and my left arm dug into her side. Every few moments, the floor over us shuddered, like someone was knocking things around. Sally shivered and twitched, so

I gripped her tighter. I was starting to freak out from the lack of light and air and entertainment options, but just as I was ready to wobble myself silly, Janelle and Thor (Scottie?) lifted the lid off and pulled us out.

So. *Ballpark Figure* was the last movie we ever made, and it was probably one of the last movies anybody ever made. It was a mixture of fiction, reality and improv, which Zapp Stillman said was pleasingly meta—we were counting on the bandanas and the army to play themselves in the story, but I was playing a fictional character, and so were Janelle and Zapp. My character was Horace Burton, the last baseball fan on Earth who had been heartbroken since the MLB shut down and who was driving his giant hot dog vehicle to try and find the world's greatest baseball players, in a kind of *Field of Dreams*-with-lunch-meat thing. Janelle was a former hot dog mascot who had turned Vegan but still wanted to keep dressing up as a hot dog, just a meatless hot dog this time. And Zapp was some kind of coach. We filmed a sequence of the three of us piling into our hot dog car, with some animated cue-card exposition, and posted it online with minimal editing, as a kind of prequel to the actual movie, which we promised would be posted live and streaming, right as it happened, on our vumble.

By the time we were ready to leave town, an hour before dawn, the *Ballpark Figure* prologue had been up for a few hours, and we had a few thousand people refreshing our vumble over and over. I had slept a few hours, but Sally hadn't slept at all and Janelle was guzzling really terrible coffee. Sally wasn't going to be in the hot dog, she was going to be one of the people filming the action from—I hoped—a safe distance, using Matt's remote-controlled camera drones, which I had insisted on. If nothing else came of this but Sally getting somewhere safe, where she could start over, I could count that the biggest win ever.

As we rolled into the middle of the street and cranked the hot dog up to its maximum speed of 50 miles per hour, I had time as I clambered out onto the outermost front reaches of the metal bun to obsess over the contradiction between Horace Burton and myself. Horace's goal, in this movie, was to take his hot dog out onto the open road and find the lost spirit of baseball. Horace didn't want any trouble—but I, meanwhile, had no goal other than trouble, and (If I were being honest) no plans after today. How was I going to play that, in a way that preserved the integrity of Horace and his innocent love of sportsmanship? In fact, I reflected as I raised a baseball and prepared to hurl it at the shaved head of the red bandana standing on the nearest corner in front of a shuttered florist, that might be the reason why people root for the comic hero after all: the haplessness. This fresh white baseball was emblazoned with a slogan about bringing back the greatest game, and the story called for Horace to toss them out as a promotional thing, and to hit a militia member in the head purely by accident. So it was important for the story that I not look as though I were aiming. But I also couldn't afford to miss. Horace is a good person who just wants to bring joy to people, and he gets caught up in a bad situation, and the moment you think Horace brought this on himself through meanness or combativeness, that's the moment you stop pulling for him. The baseball hit the teenager in the jaw, over the neatly tied red cloth that looked too big for his skinny neck, and he whipped around and fired off a few shots with his Browning Hi Performance, while also texting his comrades with his free hand.

I tried to wear a convincing look of friendly panic, like I hadn't meant to wake a thousand sleeping giants with one stray baseball, and danced around on the front of the hot dog so hard I nearly fell under the wheels. I slipped and landed on my crotch on the very tip of the hot dog, then pulled myself back up, still trying to toss out promotional baseballs and spread goodwill, and it occurred to me for the first time that I had spent so much time worrying that I was going to hurt someone by accident, it never even occurred to me that I would finally reach a point where I would decide to cause harm on purpose. Our hot dog had red bandanas chasing us, with two motorcycles and some kind of hybrid electric Jeep. I had no idea if anybody was still shooting at me, because I couldn't see anyone aiming a gun from where I stood on one foot and I couldn't see any bullets hitting anything. Until a bullet hit me in the thigh just as the hot dog swerved without slowing and we released the blow-up dolls in their makeshift baseball uniforms. The blow-up dolls flew behind us, and I saw one of them hit a motorcyclist right where the red bandana tucked under his round white helmet, so that he lost his grip on his handlebars and went somersaulting, and I felt the blood seeping through my pants like maybe it had missed a bone but hit an artery and I was cursing myself forgetting to bring a giant comedy bottle of ketchup to squirt at people, because ketchup is the most cheerful kind of fake blood, when Ricky Artesian climbed on top of the third car of by now five that were chasing us and held up a big flatscreen TV that read "YOU MADE YOUR CHOICE ROCK TIME TO PAY" and another bullet tore through my side just as the hot dog made another sharp turn and we disappeared into the tunnel from the abandoned Back Bay T extension project.

The hot dog came to a stop in a dark hutch Xed in by fallen rusted steel girders, just as one of our bready tires gave out and the whole vehicle slumped on one side, and our support crew set about camouflaging the Wienermobile with rocks and planks. Janelle climbed out of the cab and came over to show me the vumble, the insane number of hits we were getting right now and the footage in a loop of me hurling baseballs at the red bandanas, and then she noticed that I was pissing blood from my leg and my side, and started trying to get me to lie down. Just then a message came through from Sally, who was still masterminding the filming from a remote location: "theyre not taking the bait". The bandanas were staying on their side of the line and not trying to chase us into the army barricades, like we'd hoped.

I slipped out of Janelle's grasp—easy when you're as slick as I was, just then—and leapt onto

Zapp's bicycle. Before anybody could try to stop me, I was already pedaling back the way we'd come, up the ramp and out the hidden entry way that we were just in the process of sealing up, leaping through the closing exit from darkness into the light of day. I raced close enough to Ricky Artesian to make eye contact, and hurl my second-to-last baseball, absolutely coated at this point with my own blood, at his pinstripe-suited torso. And then I spun and tore off in the direction of Storrow Drive again, not looking back to see if anyone was following me, racing with my head down, on the ramp that led up to the Turnpike. My phone thrummed with messages but I ignored it. I was already reaching the top of the ramp, all thoughts of Horace Burton, and lovable fall guys in general, forgotten. The checkpoint was a collection of pale blobs at ground level, plus a swarm of men and women with bug heads rushing around tending their one statuesque mecha and a collection of mustard-colored vehicles. My eyesight was going, my concentration going with it, my feet kept sliding off the pedals, but I kept pedaling nonetheless, until I was close enough to yank out my last limited edition promotional baseball, crook my arm back and then straighten with the hardest throw of my life. Then I wiped out. I fell partway behind a concrete barrier as Ricky and the other bandanas came up the ramp into the line of fire. I saw nothing of what came next, except that I smelled smoke and cordite and glimpsed a man with the red neck-gear falling on his hands and rearing back up, before I crawled the rest of the way behind my shelter and passed out.

When I gained consciousness, I was in a prison camp, where I nearly died, first of my wounds and later of a fiendish case of dysentery like you wouldn't believe. I never saw Sally again, but I saw our last movie, once, on a stored file on someone's battered old Stackbook. (This lady named Shari had saved the edited film to her hard drive before the Internet went futz, and people had been copying *Ballpark Figure* on pinky drives and passing it around ever since, whenever they had access to electricity.) The final act of *Ballpark Figure* was just soldiers and red bandanas getting drilled by each other's bullets until they did a garishly herky-jerky slamdance, and I have to say the film had lost any narrative thread regarding Horace Burton, or baseball, or the quest to restore professional sports to America, not to mention the comedy value of all those flailing bodies was minimal at best. The movie ended with a dedication: "To Rock Manning. Who taught me it's not whether you fall, it's how you land. Love, Sally."

Acknowledgments

I've been working on *Rock Manning* on and off for ages, so I'm sure I'll forget half the people who helped me to shape it. I definitely showed an early version of this manuscript to Liz Henry, Suzanne Kleid and Rosa Maria Quiñones, and I received advice and feedback on it from a ton of other people, including Richard Nash and Jeremy Lassen. I'm also grateful to John Joseph Adams and Hugh Howey for letting me serialize a version of it in their three-part apocalyptic anthology series, and for publishing the first section in *Lightspeed Magazine*. Rich Horton generously included that same opening section in *The Best Science Fiction & Fantasy 2015*, which was a huge boost to my confidence in this material. As always, my agent Russ Galen was incredibly supportive and astute, and did the legwork to make this strange little novella into a book in its own right. My sensitivity reader, Elsa Sjunneson-Henry, went the extra mile to help me make sure this gonzo story could work for everyone. And everyone at Subterranean Press including Bill Schafer and Yanni Kuznia believed in this weird project and blew me away with their enthusiasm and professionalism, even asking for my suggestions of cover artist. (And yay, Carolyn Nowak!) And finally, my partner Annalee Newitz has been a constant source of inspiration and brilliant conversations and warmth and support and laughter, and she was there for every step of Rock Manning's journey.